JN082805

The Journey of the Lighthouse Keeper

Natsu Mikami

Beyond the cape,
overlooking the sea,
there was a lighthouse.

In the lighthouse,
there lived an old lighthouse keeper.

2

His job is to keep the light on
so that ships can sail safely
at night.

So each night,
the lighthouse keeper
wakes up and
starts working.

During the day,
he cleans the lens,
goes fishing, and
writes in his journal.

But he has become
a little tired of his job,
doing the same thing,
in the same place,
for many years.

One day, when the lighthouse keeper was about to sleep,
he heard a knock on the door.

When he opened the door,
there was a traveler, who had injured his leg.

The lighthouse keeper tended to the wounds of the traveler,
and gave him bread and fish soup.

The traveler enjoyed his meal,
and started to talk about his travels,
about all the different deserts, fields,
and towns he had been to.

The lighthouse keeper said,
"That is awesome! I haven't been on a trip in many years."

The traveler said,
"In that case, what if I stay here until my wounds recover,
and you can go out and have an adventure?"

The excited lighthouse keeper
set off on his journey.

"Let's go,
to a place with a beautiful view!"

He went to the desert.
There were no clouds in the sky
and the sand was hot and rough,
as it baked in the sun.

"What a sunny place,"
thought the lighthouse keeper.

He went to the market.
There were many people in colorful clothes,
and many things he had never seen before.

"What a lively place,"
thought the lighthouse keeper.

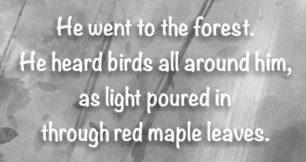

He went to the forest.
He heard birds all around him,
as light poured in
through red maple leaves.

"What a bright day,"
thought the lighthouse keeper.

He went to the meadow.
The setting sun was fading in the distance,
and a soft breeze was blowing.
The moon had risen into the sky.

"What a beautiful evening,"
thought the lighthouse keeper.

It's morning.
He washed his face with cold water from the spring.
Drops fell onto the leaves floating on the surface,
shining brightly in the morning sun.

"What a refreshing morning,"
thought the lighthouse keeper.

It's night.
The forest is dark and quiet,
and smells of dirt and grass.
He remembered the sound of wavesby the lighthouse.

"What a quiet night,"
thought the lighthouse keeper.

He went to the town.
It was already midnight,
but there were
one, two...
countless lights.

"How bright, it's like there is no nighttime here!"
thought the lighthouse keeper.

The lighthouse keeper's eyes flickered in the brightness.

"The light of the lighthouse was like a small candle
compared to these bright lights,"
he thought, and begun to feel sad.

"What's wrong?"
asked a sailor, who noticed that the lighthouse keeper looked sad.

The lighthouse keeper replied,
"I have traveled far and seen many beautiful things.
But I am worried that if I continue my journey,
it will become harder and harder
to return to my lighthouse,
because my lighthouse seems worthless."

The lighthouse keeper asked the sailor
to take him back to the lighthouse.

As he sat quietly in the ship,
the sailor told him
"The night breeze feels good."

The lighthouse keeper went outside,
and he saw...

Ah!

said the lighthouse keeper.

Across the dark sea,
he saw a large, twinkling star-like light.

"That's your lighthouse," said the sailor
"We sailors travel in the dark sea,
guided by your lighthouse."

"Welcome back!"
said the traveler
as the lighthouse keeper arrived back at the lighthouse.

The lighthouse keeper thought,
"It was a wonderful trip.
but my lighthouse is alsoa wonderful place.
There is nowhere like it."

The lighthouse keeper went back to his normal days,
which were similar, but now also different.

Laying on the grass, feeling the wind blow,
watching the white clouds drift slowly, over the shimmering sea.

Morning, noon and night,
his days are full of many colors.

The lighthouse keeper opens the window wide today,
and takes a deep breath.

"This is a beautiful view too!"
he thinks.

The lighthouse keeper's journey continues.

The journey
of the lighthouse keeper

2023 年 9 月 27 日　初版第 1 刷　発行

絵　と　文　　みかみ　なつ　Natsu Mikami

監　　修　　松本　えつを　Etsuwo Matsumoto

協　　力　　ウーマンクリエイターズバンク　Woman Creators Bank
　　　　　　〒160 - 0004　東京都新宿区四谷 1-7 装美ビル 2F・3F　　TEL：03 - 5315 - 4586
　　　　　　URL：https://www.woman-college.com/　　e-mail：info@woman-college.com

発　行　所　　株式会社 三恵社　Sankeisha Co., Ltd.
　　　　　　〒462 - 0056　愛知県名古屋市北区中丸町 2 - 24 - 1　　TEL：052 - 915 - 5211
　　　　　　URL：https://www.sankeisha.com

Ⓒ 2023 mikaminatsu / Woman Creators Bank　ISBN 978-4-86693-807-3　Printed in Japan